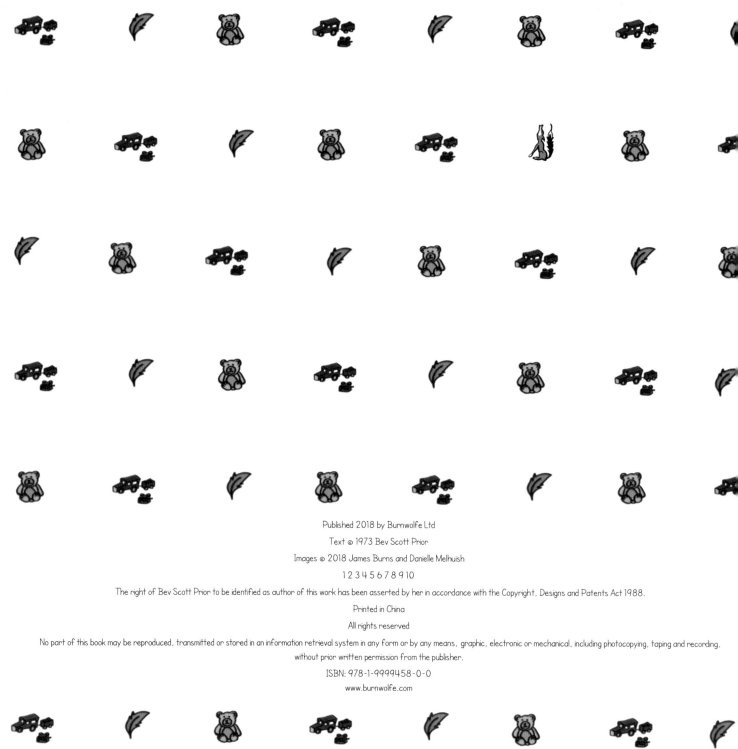

Published 2018 by Burnwolfe Ltd

Text © 1973 Bev Scott Prior

Images © 2018 James Burns and Danielle Melhuish

1 2 3 4 5 6 7 8 9 10

The right of Bev Scott Prior to be identified as author of this work has been asserted by her in accordance with the Copyright, Designs and Patents Act 1988.

Printed in China

ISBN: 978-1-9999458-0-0

www.burnwolfe.com

Benjy Bunn's
Busy Day

Benjy Bunn was in the **kitchen**,

thought he'd make Mama a **cake.**

Grabbed the **flour, eggs** and **butter,**

spied a **tin** in which to **bake.**

Couldn't find a **spoon** to mix it,

never mind this fork will **do.**

Daddy used it in the **garden,**

Benjy thought he'd use it **too!**

Soon he'd made a **lovely** mixture,
even though it did look **grey.**
"Mummy **would** be pleased," thought Benjy,
"What a **clever** Bunn" she'd **say.**

Climbed upon the chair to reach it,

knocked the icing sugar **down,**

covering the little bunny,

causing him to wear a **frown.**

'Til he **spied** himself reflected

in the window, oh, what **fun!**

Hadn't made a **cake** for Mummy,

had made himself a **Sugar Bunn!**

"Better get **cleaned up**," thought Benjy,

licked himself all **nice** and **neat.**

For, as **every** little Bunn knows,

bunnies should be clean and **sweet!**

Added **sugar** to the cake mix,
found some currants, put in **two.**
One for **Mummy,** one for **Daddy,**
Benjy thought he'd **eat** a **few.**

To tell the truth that **naughty** fellow **ate** those currants, one by **one.**

Looked inside the empty packet, saw he'd left his Mummy **none.**

"**Not** to worry," thought that bunny,

dashing through the open **door.**

With **Play-Doh** he soon came running,

"I'll soon make my Mummy **more!**"

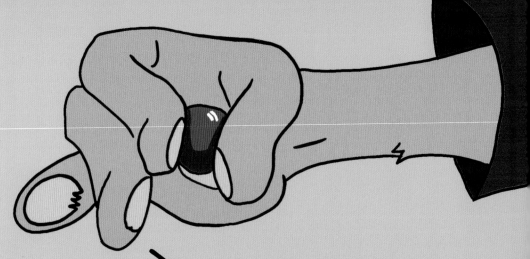

In his paps he **rolled** those `currants`,
"Mummy **will** be pleased", he **thought.**

He'd **replace** what he had eaten,

`cos he knew that's what he **ought!**

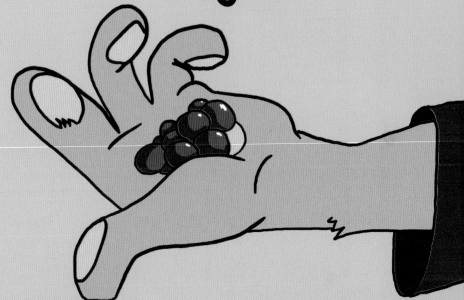

Now to put them in a packet,

he had lost the currant **box.**

Couldn't find a box or packet,

so he put them in his **socks!**

Took the socks into the larder,

pegged them up upon the **shelf,**

with a little **note** that stated,

'When you're hungry help **yourself.'**

The cake he popped into the oven,

mustn't touch the gas taps, **no!**

That's a job for **Mummy**, Bunn knew,

then **upstairs** that Bunn did **go.**

To his **bedroom** went that chappie,

I'll tidy up my room **today.**

Opened drawers and took the **clothes** out,

Mummy could **throw** those **away!**

"Next to make the **bed**," thought Benjy,

threw the pillow in the **air.**

It hit the ceiling—split right open,

floating feathers **everywhere!**

Being tidy **wasn't** easy,
helping Mummy seemed quite **hard!**
Having done his best to please her,
out went Bunn into the **yard.**

Saw Daddy's plant pots in the corner,

throw away those nasty **weeds.**

A fellow has to help his Daddy!

Oh dear, they were his Daddy's **seeds!**

Thought he'd water Daddy's garden,
turned on full the water **hose.**
In the wind blew Mummy's washing,
Naughty Bunn sprayed all the **clothes!**

They would be **just right** for ironing,

Mummy dampened clothes to **press.**

He sprinkled water on the trousers,

then he sprayed his Mummy's **dress.**

Mummy's voice was soon heard calling,

"BENJY, COME HERE RIGHT AWAY!"

"Coming Mummy," called back Bunny,

"I **have** been a **good boy** today!"

Benjy Bunn is the brainchild of Bev Scott Prior who, in 1973, wrote the first Benjy book for her children. It was to be the start of a new adventure. One story became two, and many more soon followed.

Now lovingly illustrated by her grandchildren, this delightful series continues to grow for her great-grandchildren and other young readers.

From Bev and all her family: "We hope you enjoy Benjy's adventures as much as we do!"

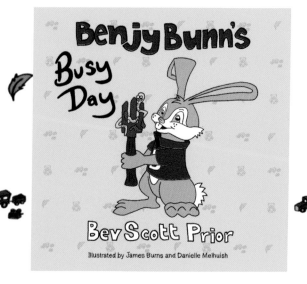

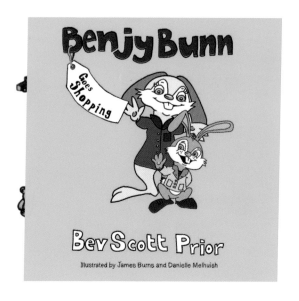